2017

Merry Christmas,
Victoria! Always be
brave!
♡ Uncle Mark
and
Auntie Nicola

be
brave
little
one

sourcebooks
jabberwocky

Written and illustrated by

Marianne Richmond

Copyright © 2017 by Marianne Richmond
Cover and internal design © 2017 by Sourcebooks, Inc.
Cover design by Brittany Vibbert/Sourcebooks, Inc.
Cover and internal illustrations © Marianne Richmond, Freepik.com

Sourcebooks and the colophon are registered trademarks of Sourcebooks, Inc.

All rights reserved. No part of this book may be reproduced in any form or by any electronic or mechanical means including information storage and retrieval systems—except in the case of brief quotations embodied in critical articles or reviews—without permission in writing from its publisher, Sourcebooks, Inc.

The characters and events portrayed in this book are fictitious and are used fictitiously. Any similarity to real persons, living or dead, is purely coincidental and not intended by the author.

Published by Sourcebooks Jabberwocky, an imprint of Sourcebooks, Inc.
P.O. Box 4410, Naperville, Illinois 60567-4410
(630) 961-3900
Fax: (630) 961-2168
www.sourcebooks.com

Library of Congress Cataloguing-in-Publication Data is on file with the publisher.

Source of Production: Worzalla, Stevens Point, WI
Date of Production: June 2017
Run Number: 5009402

Printed and bound in the United States of America.

WOZ 10 9 8 7 6 5 4 3 2 1

Dedicated to
me and to you.

When I look at you,
shining bright as the sun,
I wish for you this...

be
brave
little
one!

Be brave to begin
to listen inside
to the voice of your heart,
so truthful and wise.

How far
will I go?

What things
can I be?

When I get to *choose*
what brave is to me.

Be brave to step up
and try something new.

Be brave to step out
when it isn't for you.

Be brave
to stand up
and tell what
you know.

Be brave
to sit down
and say
a "hello."

Be brave to explore
in the daring unknown.

Be brave to return
to the cozy of home.

Be brave
to be scared,

to stomp
and to cry.

Be brave to mess up
before you retry.

Be brave to believe
in what you can't see—
with the ups and the downs
that are all meant to be.

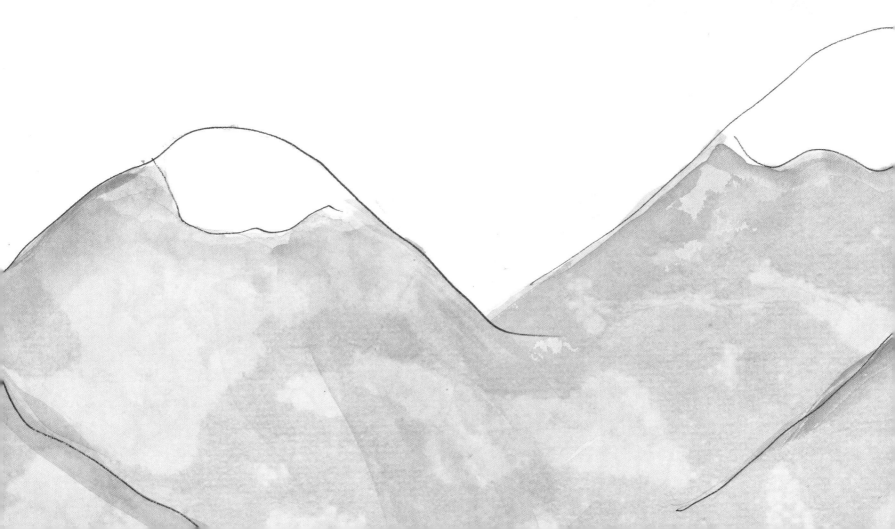

Be brave to keep going
when going is tough.

Be brave to be still
when you've had enough.

Be brave to be with your feelings, each one:

the happy and sad, the silly and glum.

Be brave
to be quiet.

Be brave
to be loud.

Be brave to achieve and be fully proud.

Be brave to BE YOU
on your journey begun.
Let your heart lead the way...

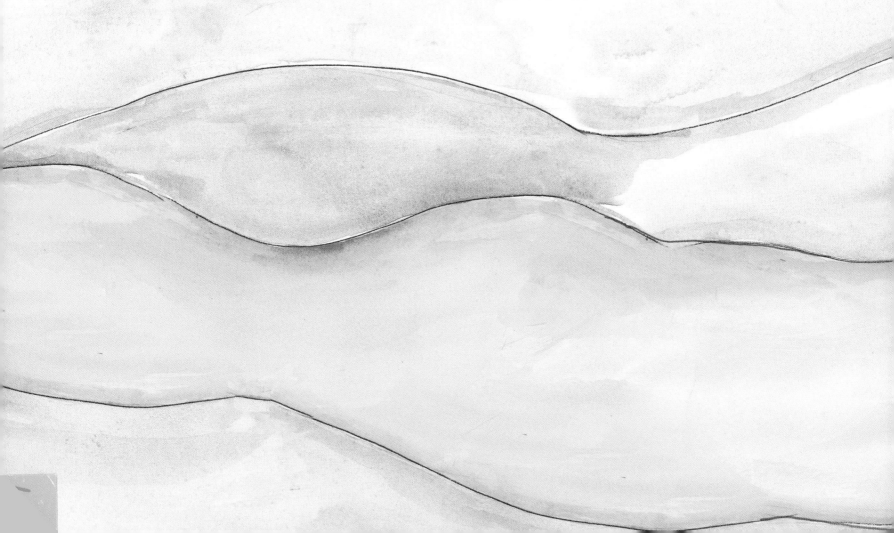

be
brave
little
one!

ABOUT THE AUTHOR

Beloved author
and illustrator
Marianne Richmond
has touched the lives
of millions for two
decades through her
heartfelt books and gifts
that help people feel their
feelings and connect with
whom they love.